# GERALD M<sup>c</sup>BOING BOING

based on the Academy Award–winning motion picture by

## Dr. Seuss

pictures adapted by MEL CRAWFORD

HarperCollins *Children's Books*

Trademark of Random House, Inc., HarperCollins Publishers Ltd, Authorised User.

1 3 5 7 9 10 8 6 4 2

ISBN: 0-00-726920-X
ISBN-13: 978-0-00-726920-4

© 1950, 1978 by Columbia Picture Industries, Inc.
A Beginner Book published by arrangement with Random House Inc., New York, USA
First published in Great Britain in 2001.
This edition published in Great Britain in 2008 by HarperCollins Children's Books.

HarperCollins Children's Books is a division of
HarperCollins Publishers Ltd, 77-85 Fulham Palace Road,
Hammersmith, London W6 8JB.

The HarperCollins website address is:
www.harpercollinschildrensbooks.co.uk

Printed and bound by Printing Express, Hong Kong

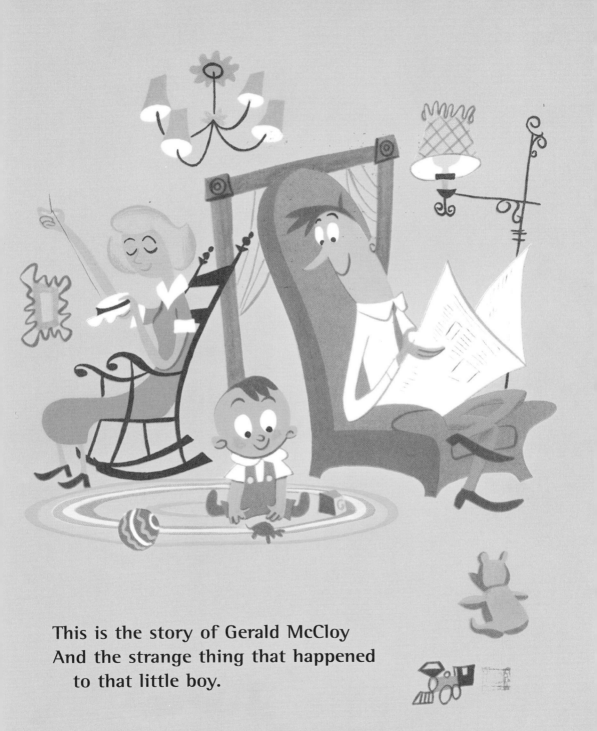

This is the story of Gerald McCloy
And the strange thing that happened
   to that little boy.

They say it all started
   when Gerald was two—
That's the age kids start talking—
   least, most of them do.
Well, when he started talking,
   you know what he said?

He didn't talk words—
   he went BOING BOING! instead!
"What's that?" cried his father,
   his face turning grey,
"That's a very odd thing
   for a young boy to say!"

And poor Gerald's father
    rushed to the phone
And quick dialled the number
    of Doctor Malone.
"Come over fast!"
    the poor father pled.
"Our boy can't speak words—
    he goes BOING BOING instead!"

"I see," said the doctor,
   "it's just as you said.
He doesn't speak words—
   he goes BOING BOING instead!

"I've no cure for this.
   I can't handle the case."
And he packed up his pills
   and walked out of the place.

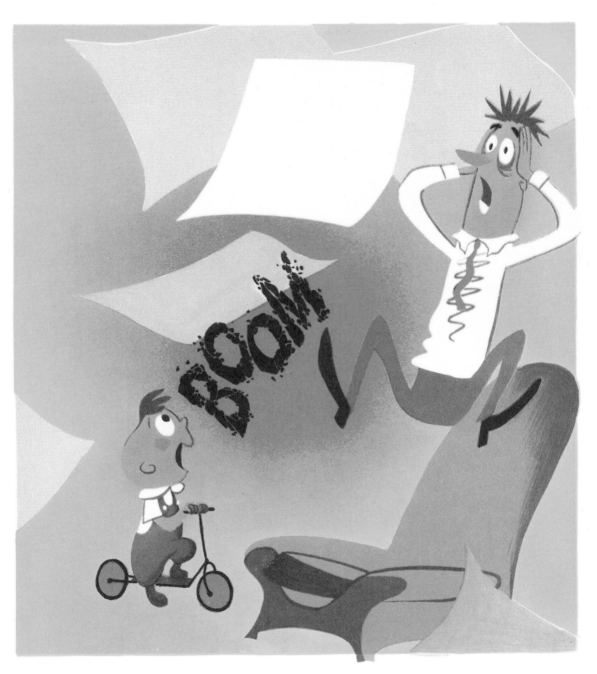

Then months passed, and Gerald
    got louder and louder
Till one day he went *BOOM!*
    like a big keg of powder!

It was then that his father
    said, "This is enough!
He'll drive us both mad
    with this terrible stuff!
A boy of his age
    shouldn't sound like a fool.
He's got to learn words.
    We must send him to school."

So Gerald marched off,
an obedient creature,

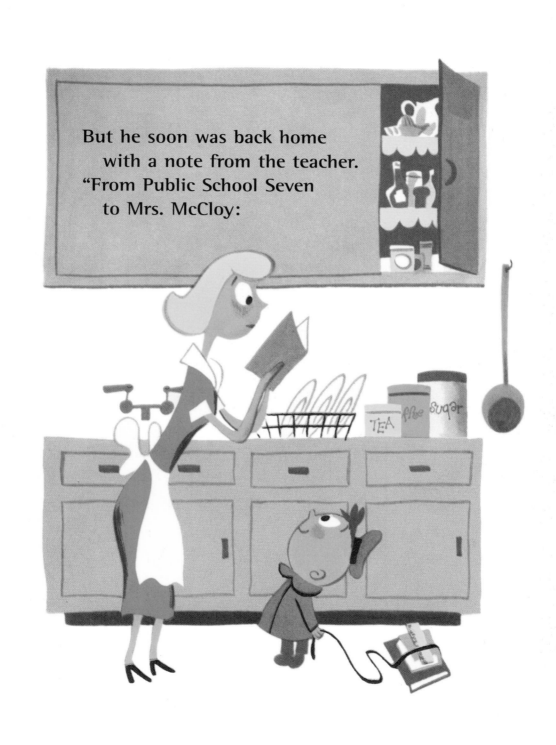

But he soon was back home
with a note from the teacher.
"From Public School Seven
to Mrs. McCloy:

Your little son Gerald's
a most hopeless boy.
We cannot accept him,
for we have a rule
That pupils must not go
Cuckoo in our school.
Your boy will go HONK
all his life, I'm afraid.
Sincerely yours, Fanny Schultz,
Teacher, First Grade."

And as little Gerald
grew older, he found
When a fellow goes **BAM!**
no one wants him around.

When a fellow goes *SKREEK!*
    he won't have any friends.
For once he says, *"CLANG CLANG CLANG!"*
    all the fun ends.

"Nyah nyah!" they all shouted,
"Your name's not McCloy!
You're Gerald McBoing Boing,
the noise-making boy!"

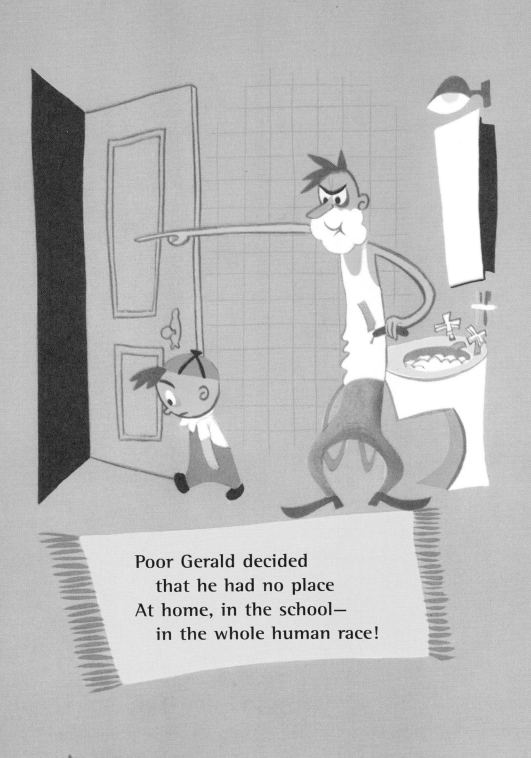

Poor Gerald decided
   that he had no place
At home, in the school—
   in the whole human race!

And so he concluded
　　that, drear and forlorn,
He would just disappear
　　in the thick of a storm.

But as he was boarding
a slow-moving freight,
A voice from the darkness
called out, "Stop, boy! Wait!"

"Aren't you Gerald McBoing Boing,
    the lad who makes squeaks?
My boy, I have searched
    for you many long weeks!
I can make you the most
    famous lad in the nation,
For I own the BONG-BONG-BONG
    Radio Station!

"I need a smart fellow
to make all the sounds,
Who can bark like a dog,
and bay like the hounds!

"Your GONG is terrific,
   your toot is inspired!
Quick come to BONG-BONG-BONG,
   McBoing Boing—you're hired!"

Now his parents, proud parents,
    are able to boast
That their Gerald's CLOP-CLOP, BANG!
    is known coast to coast.

Now Gerald is rich,
   he has friends, he's well fed,
'Cause he doesn't speak words,
   he goes BOING BOING instead!